Be the Vet

7 Dog + Cat Stories

Test Your Veterinary Knowledge

By: Dr. Ed Blesy and Marcy Blesy

Introduction

In *Be the Vet*, you will learn diagnoses for common veterinary problems. First you will read a story about a family with a dog or cat. The animal will experience a health issue, sometimes the result of an illness and sometimes the result of an emergency. You will have the opportunity to make your own notes as if you were the veterinarian diagnosing the problem and make a diagnostic plan, or treatment plan, to help the pet.

For example:

Name of the Animal (patient): Fido

Type of Animal: Dog

Symptoms or Injuries: Not eating, Difficulty walking, etc.

Treatment: Do blood work. Give medication. Take x-rays, etc.

Then you will compare your plan with that of Dr. Edmund Blesy, a licensed veterinarian with sixteen years of experience in veterinary practice. Dr. Blesy will go into more detail than you will, but writing down what you know from the story paired with your own ideas will help you learn to think like a doctor.

The diagnoses given in this book are specific to the fictional cases presented. Should your pet experience health problems, please consult your own veterinarian as each case is unique and needs its own analysis. The cases in this book are meant to give general information and educate the reader about common veterinary problems.

Table of Contents

Attack

Pawing with a *tap, tap, tap* at the back door, Heidi reminds our family that today is the first day of spring, and there are no more excuses of snow-filled mornings stopping her from getting that early morning walk with her family.

"It's your turn!" yells my brother Luke from the living room as he turns down *Sports Center* on the television.

I put on a jacket and grab Heidi's hot pink leash. Mom packs school lunches while Dad showers for work. Dog walking is one of the new chores Mom and Dad added for us. She says we need more responsibility now that we're older. I don't complain, though. I love being outside. Besides, getting a chore done before school even starts is a bonus. That means there will be more time to shoot baskets after school.

With a bag in hand for any poop accidents, I hook on Heidi's leash. She sits obediently, wagging her bushy brown tail happily, her ears alert with excitement.

"Just around the block!" yells Mom from the kitchen as I shut the front door. Everyone knows everyone in this neighborhood. Mom doesn't need to worry. The families are mostly other kids that go to school with Luke and me or grandparents that still like living in a small community. Heidi knows all of the smells of the other dogs that live around her house, but she still insists upon sniffing every fire hydrant, bush, or electrical pole she finds. I am in a hurry to finish this walk, though. I've got a science test to review for one more time before the bus comes. I decide to let Heidi off her leash on the last stretch of the sidewalk in front of our home. Dad and Mom don't know I unleash her, but it's okay. Heidi is fast even with her short legs and loves to sprint to the front door, knowing a tasty rawhide or other treat will be her reward for beating me home. At least that's what I like to think Heidi is thinking as she races full speed ahead of me. But things aren't normal today. Heidi doesn't turn toward the house when she reaches our yard. I hear the unnatural bark of my beloved dog before I see what the cause is. I see Dad run outside the front door, too. Racing toward the yard I watch as Dad tries to untangle the unfamiliar dog from Heidi. I stand by in silence not knowing how to help. A car pulls into our driveway. A man with a mustache and legs almost two times those of my dad jumps out of his car and starts yelling at the large black dog that is fighting with Heidi. The dog stops only when its owner yanks on its collar and drags it back to the car.

"Sorry, man," he says to my dad. I think my dad must be stunned because he's speechless as the man drives away without another word. I can't believe he would just leave like that.

"Heidi!" I yell as I see Dad pick her up and start walking toward the house. She's whimpering, a pathetic sound that could make a grown man cry. That includes my dad. She's bleeding from a back leg. It looks nasty. I can see muscle hanging out the wound as I draw near.

"Tell your mom to call the vet. We'll meet him at the office."

"Dad, will she be okay?" I ask, scared of the answer.

"That's why we're going to see the veterinarian," he says.

"And get me an old blanket for the backseat."

"I'm coming, too!" I yell as I run in the house to find Mom. And I know he'll let me. He has to. It was all my fault. I never should have taken Heidi off the leash.

Mom lays the blanket out on the backseat of Dad's car. Luke talks to Heidi the whole time while Mom and Dad talk privately, I suppose about whether or not to let me miss school to go to the veterinary clinic.

"It's okay, Heidi," Luke says. "You're going to be fine, old girl." He has tears in his eyes. I feel worse. I can't believe I let this happen.

I sit in the backseat with Heidi while Dad drives. She's panting with short breaths, her eyes bulging like she's stressed. I don't know what else to do but to gently pat her shoulders trying to calm her.

The vet and his vet tech meet us at the door of the veterinary clinic. Dad lays Heidi on an exam table. I stand back in the room, not wanting to get in the way. She's not making any more whimpering sounds, just heavy breathing. The blood is still thick, entangled in the hair that surrounds the wound. I've been in the clinic before, usually when Heidi needs shots or to get tick and flea medicine, but I've never been here for an emergency.

*****

If you were the veterinarian, what would you do next? Make a list of Heidi's injuries. Then make a diagnostic (treatment) plan based upon the information that you have. When you are done, read what the veterinarian will do.

Name of the Animal (patient):

Type of Animal:

Symptoms or Injuries:

Treatment:

History:

*Heidi was bitten by another dog.

*Only one wound is seen.

Assessment:

*First assess Heidi's general condition.

*Is she alert and responsive?

*What is her respiration rate (breathing rate)?

*Check her mucous membrane color (the tissue in the gums of her mouth).

Since Heidi appears alert, she has a normal respiratory rate, and her mucous membranes are pink, it was determined she was not in shock. Therefore, there is not an urgent need to support her care with oxygen, fluids, or a warming system to raise her temperature.

*Assess the wound and other potential injuries.

*Most bite wounds are not life-threatening. If there are deep penetrating wounds to the thorax (upper body) or abdomen (belly), they can cause more problems. Heidi's most significant wound appears to be confined to one area of the leg. There are many other small puncture wounds caused by the dog bites.

*The wound characteristics will determine what type of anesthesia will be needed. Anesthesia is medicine given to put the animal to sleep temporarily while surgery is performed. The type of wound will also determine what surgical technique and materials are needed to close it up.

*Heidi's wound looks worse that it is. Sometimes even small wounds can bleed a lot.

TIP: Always check carefully for other wounds. They can be difficult to see if the hair coat is thick.

Treatment Plan:

*This patient is placed under anesthesia. This is done so Heidi does not feel the surgery to repair the large wound. The small puncture wounds will not need to be surgically closed.

*The hair around the wound is clipped and cleaned. Antiseptic solution is used to decrease the amount of bacteria in the wound that could make the dog sicker by causing an infection. Analgesics (pain medications) are given.

*The wound is closed in multiple layers with suture material. Some of the sutures will absorb under the skin as the wound heals. Other sutures that are placed in the skin will need to be removed in 10-14 days.

*It is good that Heidi is up-to-date on rabies vaccination. Since we do not know the rabies vaccination of the dog that bit her, Heidi will need a booster vaccination and observation for a period of time. A vaccination is a medication given to help prevent disease. Rabies is a disease that can cause death in dogs, humans, and other animals and can be passed on through a bite.

*Heidi will be sent home with oral pain medication (to be taken by mouth) and antibiotics. Antibiotics are medications used in a case like this to help the body fight off bacterial organisms introduced by the dog bite.

*****

Heidi has been home for a week now. She is doing so much better. Her leg is healing nicely. I got in big trouble for letting Heidi off her leash. No video games for a whole week! I understand, though. I put Heidi's life in danger. Thankfully we haven't seen that black dog again, but I'm still careful when I take Heidi on her walks, *with her leash*.

The vet wants to see Heidi one more time to make sure her wound is healing nicely. Then she should be good as new. And nothing shows me more that Heidi has forgiven me than those big sloppy kisses she greets me with each morning. There's no better wake-up call.

Toxic

"Stop running in the house!" yells Mom as I chase my little sister up the stairs and back down in a heated game of morning tag before church. Megan's wearing some froo-froo fancy dress with sparkles on the top. I have to dress up, too. I hate dressing up. But it's Easter, and Mom insists we wear only the finest clothes for Sunday morning church on this special day of the year.

"Have you seen the cat?" asks Mom. "I can't find her anywhere."

"I haven't seen her," says Megan. I shake my head *no*.

"Go look in your closets, okay?" Mom asks. "Your Dad opened the door to get the paper this morning. You know she's not an outside cat. Please help me find her."

Mom looks worried. Luna is her first baby she's always told us. She's fifteen which is a whole lot older than Megan and me.

"Sure, we'll look for her, Mom." Megan and I decide to split up. I take the second floor. Megan checks

16

the main floor. I look through Megan's closet, tossing her dolls and dress-up clothes aside. Sometimes Luna hides in the back of the closet in a nest of doll blankets. She's not there today. I look through my closet, too, which doesn't take very long. I'm the neat one in the family. Dad is still upstairs. I think he likes stressing Mom out by getting ready for church at the last minute.

I'm about to give up when I hear a noise coming from the upstairs bathroom. I go inside. Luna is lying on a towel that fell from the towel bar. She's lurching like she's getting ready to vomit. Her body is shaking. She doesn't look well.

"*Mom!*" I yell. "Come here!" Mom runs upstairs, joined by Dad who is wearing a fancy suit, like the kind he wears to weddings.

"What's going on?" he asks. But he doesn't need an answer. Luna is throwing up again. She looks so pitiful sitting on the bathroom mat. Her eyes look up at me as if she is saying, *"Help me."* But she doesn't make a single sound.

17

"*What's wrong?*" asks Megan, her eyes big with surprise when she sees Luna. She starts crying. Mom shoos her out of the room. Dad leans over Luna and pets her.

"What did she get in to?" asks Mom pointing at Luna's vomit. Dad takes a closer look.

"It looks like a leaf, but we don't have any plants." It's true. Mom can't keep a plant alive even if her life depends upon it. But they're wrong.

"We do," I whisper. They turn to look at me.

"What do you mean?" asks Dad.

"The Easter lily." Mom and I say it at the same time. Megan's best friend gave everyone in her class an Easter lily at school on Friday. It's sitting on the entertainment center in the living room. Without being asked, I run down the stairs. The green leafy stem stands tall with the blooming white flowers opened wide toward the sun shining in the window. I examine the lily closer. Little bits of leaf are missing as is part of the white flower turned closest to the window.

"Luna's been eating the Easter lily!" I yell. Without even answering back Mom's on the phone.

"Who's she calling?" asks Megan as I rejoin my family upstairs.

"The veterinarian," Dad tells Megan.

"Does Luna have to go the doctor?" she asks.

"That's what Mom is trying to..." but he doesn't get a chance to finish.

"Everyone get in the car *now*," says Mom urgently. "Easter lilies can be toxic," she says.

"What's that mean?" Megan asks.

"It means they are poisonous," I tell her.

*****

If you were the veterinarian, what would you do next? Make a list of Luna's injuries. Then make a diagnostic (treatment) plan based upon the information that you have. When you are done, read what the veterinarian will do.

Name of the Animal (patient):

Type of Animal:

Symptoms or Injuries:

Treatment:

Lilies can damage Luna's kidneys. This is an emergency situation. The outcome can be as severe as death.

History:

*With the detailed history, the diagnosis of lily toxicity is easy in this case.

Assessment:

*Luna appears normal at this time but requires immediate treatment.

Treatment Plan:

*Since the owner noted that Luna vomited at home, an emetic is not needed. An emetic is a medication given to make an animal vomit. This is done for some toxic substances if recently swallowed. By causing an animal to vomit, the toxin's harmful effect can be lessened.

*Activated charcoal is a medication that can be given to decrease the absorption of the toxin (poison) from the intestines.

*An intravenous catheter will be placed. This is a device placed in the vein to help when giving fluids and medicines to the animals. The catheter will be used to aggressively give fluids over multiple days.

*Blood samples will be taken now and in 48 hours. This is done to help monitor the health of the patient. The doctor would be checking to see if the kidneys are functioning properly.

FACT: Peace lily and lily of the valley are not true lilies. These plants do not cause kidney problems in cats.

FACT: Dogs do not tend to have as much of a problem with these plants. They tend to have mild, short-term gastrointestinal upset. This includes vomiting and diarrhea.

*****

Luna is back to her normal, naughty self. She paws at the couch. She kicks litter everywhere. She tries to sneak outside every time someone opens the front door. But no matter how much trouble she causes I am so happy to have her home. We are lucky we had not left for church when Luna got into the Easter lily. Learning about poisonous plants was an important lesson we will never forget.

Ouch!

It's the first day of summer vacation, and I'm already bored. Grandma is teaching my older brother how to make spaghetti sauce from scratch. I say, *"What's the point? Isn't that why we have grocery stores?"* At least I have Bo. He's been our dog since I was a baby. Mom told me that when she brought me home from the hospital, Bo wouldn't leave my side. When I cried he'd lick my face to comfort me. I'm not sure that would work today. That's actually kind of gross, but I know Bo loves me.

"Come here, Bo." Bo walks over to me in my bedroom. He doesn't run too much anymore. He sits looking at me as if he's saying, *"What now? I was taking a nap."* He's such a good dog, though. "Want to play catch, old boy?" He starts wagging his tail, and his tongue hangs out the side of his mouth. It looks like a *yes* to me.

For fifteen minutes I toss the red rubber ball out my bedroom door and down the hall. Bo retrieves it each time, even running to get it a couple of times. He could stand to lose a few pounds, so the exercise is good for him. It's times like this, though, that I wished I lived in town so I could walk over to a friend's house to play. The summer will seem way too long if Bo is my only company, no matter how much I love him.

"Lunch is ready," Grandma says from the kitchen. Well, at least the homemade sauce should *taste* good even if it seems like way too much trouble for me to bother with.

After lunch, Grandma makes my brother and I ride bikes down our long driveway. If this is her idea of fun she's wrong, but it is nice to get out of the house. When we return to the house Grandma is waving her hands wildly while calling us. We drop our bikes on the ground and go running to her.

"What's the matter, Grandma?" we ask.

"I was trying to take Bo for a walk," she says, "but he won't budge. Here, watch." Grandma attaches Bo's leash to his collar. "Come, Bo. Let's go for a walk." Bo looks up at Grandma with the same expression I gave her when she asked me to make homemade spaghetti sauce, kind of like, *"Are you crazy?"* I take a turn. I get down low, so he knows I'm speaking just to him.

"Hey, Bo. Want to go for a walk, old buddy? You can have a tasty treat when we get back." Bo perks up at the words *tasty treat*. His ears stand up straight. I have to tug on the leash a little to get Bo to budge. He seems to have trouble getting up.

"What's wrong with his back leg?" asks Grandma. I look at Bo who is now standing next to me. His right back leg is slightly off the ground like he's trying not to put any weight on it.

"Come, Bo." I pull the leash gently towards the door. Bo moves but doesn't put his back leg on the ground. He is clearly limping. "I think we should call the veterinarian," I say. Grandma nods her head *yes*.

*****

If you were the veterinarian, what would you do next? Make a list of Bo's injuries. Then make a diagnostic (treatment) plan based upon the information that you have. When you are done, read what the veterinarian will do.

Name of the Animal (patient):

Type of Animal:

Symptoms or Injuries:

Treatment:

History:

*The lameness (sore leg which makes walking difficult) was sudden and not gradual when it started. This helps to tell the difference between possible causes of lameness. Example: arthritis versus muscle or ligament injury.

*Has there been any history of yelping or crying out in pain?

*Has it been harder for Bo to do stairs, jump, or get up over the last year?

FACT: A dog's age needs to be considered as a diagnosis is determined. Senior dogs (older dogs) are more likely to develop certain conditions that lead to lameness. For example, dogs are more likely to have a ligament injury or arthritis problems as they age.

Assessment:

*The doctor watches Bo walk around the exam room. This helps to confirm the leg having a problem. It also helps to give a clue as to how serious the injury is.

*The doctor palpates (feels) and manipulates (moves the joints of the leg where the bones connect) the good leg and then the lame leg. The exam starts at the nails and moves up the leg.

*Bo's knee was checked for a ligament tear. The test is called a "cranial drawer" test. The doctor checks for increased movement in the joint. The test for Bo was negative.

*After a thorough exam, the doctor suspects that Bo has arthritic hips. Radiographs (x-rays) were offered to the client to confirm the diagnosis.

Treatment Plan:

*The doctor stresses that is very important for Bo to lose weight. Excess weight creates additional stress on joints and ligaments.

*The doctor recommends a dietary supplement that will help the joints be less painful. This is a very safe way to help reduce some pain in the affected joints.

*It is important for the owner to make sure Bo gets exercise. The exercise should not be too aggressive.

Walking is ideal. This is needed to make sure the muscles are kept strong to help support the sore joints.

*Certain medications are recommended for Bo. They will take some of the pain away immediately.

FACT: Sometimes surgery is recommended for dogs with lameness issues. It may be suggested when arthritis is severe or if there is a ligament injury.

*****

We've been following the vet's recommendations perfectly. Mom set up a chart showing that twice a day Bo gets a short walk. We all take turns. I do wish I could still play catch with Bo, but I'm just happy he's here to curl up with me every night and keep me company when I'm watching television. He's long past his crazy puppy years Mom described, but he's a loyal member of the family. Can you ask for anything more?

Thirsty

Mom always told me that I could get a cat when we moved to town. I just didn't know that the cat would find *me* instead of *me* finding the cat. That's what happened with Jingle. She started living with us last winter. The first big snowstorm of the year was blowing and drifting outside our house. I had just put one ice cube in the toilet because someone told me once if I did that we might get a snow day. I didn't really believe that, of course, but it was worth a try. I could barely make out the streetlights in front of our house. I opened the front door to get a better look at the action whirling around our house. Mom started shouting about me letting all the cold air inside. I was about to close the door when I heard a sound. It sounded like bells jingling over and over. I wiped the snow off my glasses and peered into the cold night. I heard the sound again. *Jingle. Jingle. Jingle.* I ran back inside to get my boots, gloves, hat, and coat.

"I'll be right back," I'd said to my mom. Sure enough that sound was still there when I stood outside on my front porch. It was coming from behind a row of bushes to the right of the porch. I stomped toward the bushes. Out from behind the second bush came the *jingle, jingle, jingle.* A little black kitten wearing a tiny collar and one tinier bell latched around its neck peeked at me. She froze, and not because of the cold temperatures. She was frightened. But as soon as I reached my hand out to pet her, she relaxed her body. Her head rubbed against my leg, and every time she moved she'd sound like church bells.

Dad helped me put up signs around town and in the newspaper with Jingle's picture, but nobody claimed her. Maybe Santa dropped her off as an early Christmas present. I'll never know because she's been ours for a year now.

Today I'm trying to do my homework with Jingle curled up in my lap. She feels thinner when I pet her. She's not purring, either. In fact, she hasn't purred much at all the last few weeks. Maybe she's sick. When I get up to put my homework in my book bag, Jingle walks slowly to her water bowl. She stands there for a really long time drinking water. I remember that Mom commented last night that Jingle was drinking a lot of water lately. I wonder why.

"Don't forget to finish your chores before you play video games," says Mom. I finally finished my homework, and now I have to do my chores, not my favorite time of the day. *Ugh.*

I put away the laundry that is piled on my bed. How could one kid have so many dirty clothes? Then I go to the basement to scoop out Jingle's litter box. There are *a lot* of litter clumps. I mean *a lot,* like Jingle has been peeing all day. It's been like this the last week or so. I need to remember to tell Mom and Dad. I wonder if that's normal. I guess it makes sense. She drinks more, so she goes to the bathroom more.

"Mom, I'm done with my chores," I say. "Can I play video games now?"

"Sure. Go ahead," says Mom. I turn on the Xbox and look through my games to find the one I want to play. I can't stop thinking about Jingle, though.

"Hey, Mom, can you give Jingle extra food for dinner tonight? She looks thinner, and I think maybe she needs to eat more."

"The opposite is true. I've been feeding her more the last few weeks. I've had the same thought as you," she says.

"Maybe we should call the veterinarian," I say.

"That's a good idea," says Mom. "We'll get Jingle an appointment for this week. Don't worry." But I do worry. What could be wrong with Jingle?

*****

If you were the veterinarian, what would you do next? Make a list of Jingle's injuries. Then make a diagnostic (treatment) plan based upon the information that you have. When you are done, read what the veterinarian will do.

Name of the Animal (patient):

Type of Animal:

Symptoms or Injuries:

Treatment:

History:

*Jingle is drinking and urinating more than usual.

*Jingle is losing weight, but her appetite has been normal.

*Jingle may have less energy than usual.

Assessment:

*Every pet is weighed when it comes in for a physical exam. Jingle has lost over 4 pounds in less than a year.

*There are no other significant findings on the physical exam.

Plan:

*Laboratory tests are needed to find out what is wrong with Jingle.

*Urinalysis is a test on urine. Since Jingle will not urinate in a cup for the doctor, a procedure with a needle and syringe is used to take urine directly out of the bladder (where the urine is stored in the abdomen). The lab test on the urine shows that Jingle is losing large amounts of glucose (sugar) in her urine. The urine is also much more dilute (or clear in color) than it should be.

*A sample of blood is taken from Jingle. This blood can tell the doctor about many things going on inside the patient's body. In this case, the glucose level in the blood tests very high.

*A diagnosis of diabetes can be made. Diabetes is a disease whereby the body is unable to use the energy from foods normally. The blood sugar level gets very high. It is lost by the body into the urine.

Treatment:

*A medication called insulin will have to be given twice every day to Jingle. This will help her body so she can use and control her glucose levels.

*Jingle will be placed on a high protein canned food diet. This helps Jingle naturally control her glucose.

FACT: Diabetes, kidney problems, and hyperthyroidism (problem with a gland that produces a substance needed for normal body functions) are the three most common diseases that cause cats to drink and urinate more than usual.

*****

Jingle is doing much better. I'm glad Dad isn't afraid of needles like I am. He gives Jingle two shots of insulin every day to help control her glucose levels. After the first day Jingle caught onto Dad. She'd run and hide under my bed. Because I'm the only one brave enough (and small enough) to go under my bed, I sometimes have to drag her out and hold her tight while she gets her insulin. I pet her gently and tell her we are only doing this to help make her better. I have no doubt she understands me because she only puts up a fight once in a while now. I'm grateful for the treatment. She's part of our family.

Leftovers

It's my favorite time of year, Thanksgiving. Grandma and Grandpa invite the whole family over for the celebration. Grandma makes the best turkey in the world, and Grandpa makes a killer pumpkin pie. I think it's the extra dash of cinnamon that he adds that makes the pie so memorable. Just thinking about it makes my mouth water.

My cousins, aunts, and uncles come, too. If the weather is just right we play a wild game of flag football before we eat. Like we need something to do to work up an appetite- *not!* It's really fun until my older cousin Henry pummels me into the ground which happens at least once a year despite the *no tackle* rule. He's such a brat. If he gets caught, which I will make sure happens this time, he'll have to sit at the little kids' table. There are only four seats at the adult table with room for the big kids, and five of us are considered big kids now. Yes, Henry is *not* going to sit at the adult table even if I have to take a header to insure that.

"Ready to be demolished?" Henry yells as he tosses me the football.

"I'm ready." I smile. Uncle Tom and Aunt Cheryl gather up the rest of our large family. They appoint themselves as team captains which is fine by me. They are the fairest relatives I have. They don't have any kids so they aren't as concerned with playing favorites like my aunts or uncles with kids or even my own parents, for that matter.

The first play of the game I take a long pass from Uncle Dave. Well, I almost take it because just as I reach out my hands to snag the ball Grandpa lets the dog out in the yard. Old Brownie's never seen a ball he doesn't think is for him. Who cares if it's oblong shaped and wouldn't fit in his mouth? I go tripping over the overweight hairy beast and land face first in Grandma's rose bushes that line the backyard field. I hear laughter as Henry jogs over to me.

"Priceless, dude. That roll and tumble was *priceless*."

"Shut up, Henry," I say. Aunt Cheryl tells me to go inside and find my mother. Apparently there's some blood on my hand. Yes, I screamed like a baby when I went down, but has anyone landed on the thorns of a rosebush and *not* wailed?

The activity in the house is as busy as that in the backyard. Grandma is giving orders like a captain in the army. *"Turn the oven up." "Peel more potatoes." "Where is my meat thermometer?"* I think Mom's happy to have something else to do even if it's locating a bandage for my hand.

"Stay out of the kitchen," she whispers. "Grandma's mood is on overdrive." I nod my head.

I'm not going back outside. That's for sure. I don't need any *you're a baby* comments. Plus, my hand really does hurt, not to mention my arm and back from my not-so-graceful landing. I go into the living room to watch the first televised football game of the day. Chicago is playing Detroit. I sit in Grandpa's easy chair because it's the only time I can get away with that. Right now Grandpa is the star running back for the opposing team in the backyard. You'd never know he was sixty-years-old. I stretch out my legs on the footrest when I hear the backdoor opening. *Oh no!* Here comes Brownie. Grandpa only shares his chair with Brownie, so I know what's next.

I let him lick my face because that's what Grandpa would do, but *yuck!* His energy level isn't what it used to be, though, so Brownie snuggles into my body using my legs as his pillow. Actually, I don't mind. Watching the Bears score the first touchdown in the game with a big lug of a dog sitting comfortably on my lap and no annoying cousins screaming in my ear is a pretty nice start to my Thanksgiving.

The chaos of the kitchen meets the craziness of the backyard football game when everyone gathers in the dining room. Mom directs me to the adult table. She doesn't have to say a word. I know I've earned one of those spots today because of my injury. Plus, Uncle Dave is shooing Henry to the kids' table despite his arguments against it.

"You cannot shove Mira to the ground because you don't agree with her cheerleading," I hear him saying. Wow, that's pretty low, even for Henry. I can't help but smile.

Grandpa says grace. We dive in. Everything tastes delicious. I eat slowly to savor every taste: stuffing, mashed potatoes, green bean casserole, and Grandma's turkey. I guess she found her meat thermometer because it tastes perfect.

After the kitchen is returned to tip-top shape, most of my relatives leave. They all live close by and aren't spending the night. My family lives three hours away, so we always get to spend a little extra time with Grandma and Grandpa. I love it. Once the house is quiet Grandma relaxes *a lot*. We do big puzzles with like 1000 pieces. Grandpa grumbles that we're never going to finish before Christmas, but he always adds a few pieces of his own. Mom and Dad sometimes leave me there for a few hours while they start their Christmas shopping. More and more stores are opening on Thanksgiving Day. That's just not right if you ask me.

"What's wrong with Brownie?" asks Grandpa from the kitchen. "He's not eating his food in his bowl."

"That's odd," says Grandma. "That dog never turns down a meal." We turn back to the puzzle. I find the piece that completes the horse that pulls the sleigh. I love winter puzzles. The snow pieces are always a challenge.

A half hour later I hear whimpering. Brownie is standing at the back door waiting to be let outside. If a dog could look sad, this is what his face would look like. Poor

Brownie. Something's not right. I open the door for him to go outside.

"Follow him, will you, please?" asks Grandma. "See what he does out there." I slip on my tennis shoes, turn on the patio light, and step outside. Brownie usually runs to the corner of the yard to do his business, but tonight he's barely off the patio when he squats down. *Uh-oh*. We have a problem.

The next two hours Brownie's going in and out of the house with diarrhea. Grandpa takes him out now. I can tell he's worried.

"There's blood in his poop," Grandpa tells us. "Could he have gotten into anything today with all those kids running around? Do you think someone fed him table scraps?"

"I suppose it's possible," Grandma says. Then I see her eyes get real big.

"What's wrong, Grandma?" I ask.

"Go into the pantry. Open the trash." I do as she says, but I'm not even one foot into the pantry when I see that the garbage can has been tipped over.

"The trash is all over the floor," I say.

"The turkey bones," Grandma says.

"Call the vet," says Grandpa.

*****

If you were the veterinarian, what would you do next? Make a list of Brownie's injuries. Then make a diagnostic (treatment) plan based upon the information that you have. When you are done, read what the veterinarian will do.

Name of the Animal (patient):

Type of Animal:

Symptoms or Injuries:

Treatment:

History:

*The owner mentions that Brownie got into the garbage.

*He has been having diarrhea with blood and mucous (looks like snot).

*He is not wanting to eat his food.

Assessment:

*Brownie looks lethargic (tired and slow) sitting in the exam room. Usually he is jumping all over anyone that enters the room.

*His mucous membranes (gums) are pink. They do not feel moist. This indicates Brownie may be slightly dehydrated. This can be explained by Brownie losing some bodily fluid through the diarrhea. If he also feels sick, he may not be drinking as much water as he usually does.

*The doctor feels Brownie's belly. He is attempting to identify any painful areas. He also is trying to detect objects that may be caught in the intestines or stomach.

*Temperature is 101.7 degrees.

FACT: The normal temperature for dogs is 100 to 102.5 degrees. The normal temperature for a human is 98.6 degrees.

*The doctor offered Brownie a treat. He eagerly ate this treat in the exam room.

Treatment Plan:

*The owner is instructed to feed Brownie a bland diet over the next few days. The owners may feed boiled chicken or boiled hamburger mixed with cooked rice to Brownie. If the owner prefers, they can buy a bland, balanced prescription food from the veterinary clinic. The bland food should be easy for Brownie's stomach and intestines to digest.

*Small amounts of food and water should be offered to Brownie at one time. Larger amounts may cause vomiting from a stomach that is upset.

*The doctor prescribes a medication to help clear the blood and mucous in the diarrhea.

*Blood work will be considered if Brownie's signs continue or if he starts to act worse. Pancreatitis, or an inflamed pancreas, is a serious and common condition brought on by garbage feeding. This can also be tested for through the blood. Blood work can also rule out many other serious conditions that can cause vomiting or diarrhea.

*X-rays can be used if Brownie's signs persist or worsen. This may help identify something caught in his stomach or intestines.

*The doctor also suggests an intestinal parasite screen. This is a test done on the feces (Brownie's poop) to check for parasites that may be living in his intestines. These parasites can cause diarrhea.

FACT: There tends to be more cases of gastrointestinal upset (upset stomach symptoms) during the holiday season. Food trimmings and human treats like chocolate are more available around the house.

*****

I called Grandma last night. She told me Brownie was back to his normal self after another day of upset stomach symptoms and a few days of a bland diet. She teased that Grandpa wasn't letting *all those crazy kids* back in the house again, but I know better. He acts tough, but next to Grandma his *crazy* grandkids are at the top of his favorite's list. Of course, Brownie's on that list, too. I'm pretty sure we'll all be extra careful the next time we celebrate together. And I've decided to hold Henry to blame for any future problems, real or imaginary. Why not? That's what cousins are for anyway.

Bugs

Our new puppy Sheba is the friendliest dog one would ever meet. From the minute my mom locked eyes with her in the local shelter two weeks ago when we started our search for our family's first dog, I knew she was the one. Sheba is a mutt, the best kind of dog to own, my dad said. She's a mixture of many different breeds of dogs. Other than when Sheba's following mom around the house or sniffing other dogs on walks around the block, or starting games of tag with bigger dogs at the dog park, she's curled up on my bed snoring away.

For example, this week alone she's been on two walks, run wild at the dog park, and visited our local pet store for treats. She's never met a stranger, of the two *or* four-legged kind. And for some reason every person and every pet that she meets knows she means no harm. Even crabby Mr. Lemon that lives down the street calls out to Sheba every time she passes by his prized flower garden and not in a *you'd better stay off my lawn* kind of way.

But something's not right. Sheba isn't lying in an exhausted lump at the end of my bed today. She's pacing around the living room stopping to chew on her legs. I can tell she's uncomfortable.

"What's the matter, girl?" I ask. She flinches when I pet her. I look at Sheba again. There's a bare spot near her hips where there used to be a thick patch of rust-colored fur. No wonder she looks miserable. Sheba raises her paw and chews on her leg again. Another tuft of fur flies in the air. My first thought is fleas, but it's only because my best friend's dog once had fleas. They had to wash tons of stuff in their house like blankets and sheets and carpets. It was a big pain. Sheba looks up at me with her big brown eyes and whimpers. I feel sorry for her, but the idea of fleas in the house isn't too appealing, either.

"I know, girl," I say. "Dad will call the vet. You'll be fine before you know it." I scratch behind my ear. I can't help it. Just the thought of bugs makes me itchy all over. I sure hope the veterinarian can tell us what's wrong.

*****

If you were the veterinarian, what would you do next? Make a list of Sheba's injuries. Then make a diagnostic (treatment) plan based upon the information that you have. When you are done, read what the veterinarian will do.

Name of the Animal (patient):

Type of Animal:

Symptoms or Injuries:

Treatment:

History:

*The patient, Sheba, is itchy.

*She is losing hair in multiple places. Most of the hair loss is occurring around the hip region.

*Sheba is a new pet for this family. She has not been on any tick or flea preventive medication that would decrease her chances of ticks or fleas.

Assessment:

*A simple device called a flea comb is used to help the doctor's assistant check for fleas and flea dirt. Flea dirt, or flea poop, is the dark crumbs found on a flea-covered dog. It is the waste product remaining after a flea takes and digests a blood meal. One can confirm dark debris is flea dirt if it turns red on a damp towel. Flea dirt was seen on Sheba. Upon closer inspection, the veterinarian was able to identify multiple fleas on Sheba.

Treatment Plan:

*Sheba is given a medication by mouth that will kill any fleas that are on her.

*The owner is to give a bath at home.

*After Sheba is dry, the owner will apply a topical flea preventative that the veterinarian prescribes. This medicine will protect Sheba from any new fleas that attempt to get on her.

*The owner is instructed to apply a flea preventative year-round to Sheba. She is also instructed on how to clean items at home where numerous flea eggs have fallen off of Sheba.

Fact: Dogs and cats can get tapeworms by eating fleas. Tapeworms are a type of parasite that benefits from living inside the dog's intestine. Children can get tapeworm if a dog bites a flea and then licks a child in the face.

Fact: A single flea can lay about 50 eggs in one day.

*****

Sheba is finally clean, and all of the fleas are gone. We took her back to see the vet yesterday. He said she looked clear now. Thank goodness. She's not scratching so much anymore, and we don't have to keep cleaning everything in our house. You never realize how many blankets and rugs you have in the house until your pet is diagnosed with fleas, and the laundry piles up. That's what Mom said anyway. We don't worry anymore when we have Sheba around other dogs now which is a good thing because there's no way we could keep Sheba separated from all of her friends at the dog park. Pets are a lot of work, but she's worth it.

Enemies

"Stop it! *Stop it right now!*" I hear my older sister yelling. *Oh no.* The cats must be at it again. Mom told her it was a bad idea to allow Scooter into our house, but ever since he showed up on our front steps for the first time a couple of months ago I knew it was a given: That orange and white, mean-looking, and meaner-acting cat was going to end up as our pet no matter what Mom said. Sarah always gets her way.

She *does* have a big heart, though. That's why our house has become the local neighborhood shelter for various animals over the years. Once she nursed a squirrel abandoned by its mother by using her doll's baby bottle to squeeze milk into its mouth. Another time she housed a bird with a broken wing inside her miniature dollhouse master bedroom and fed it crackers and worms from the doll's nightstand. Can you just imagine the mess? Every day after school Sarah would take the bird outside hoping its wing had healed enough for it to fly. And, finally, one day it did. Do you know that the bird still comes back every spring and eats from our bird feeder? That's what Sarah says anyway. I don't know how she really knows it's the same bird, but she thinks she knows everything.

So when Scooter (which she named her latest rescue because he always scoots away from people when they try to pet it) showed up begging for food, I knew my sister would find a way to convince Mom to let him in the house. Of course I didn't think it was a good idea, either. We already have two cats: Mr. Snooze, whose favorite activity is sleeping, and Tippy, who has three legs, after Dad backed over her with the car (putting an end to outside cats). Scooter isn't the *get along well with others* kind of cat. Everyone knows it. Case in point: My sister is constantly breaking up fights instigated by Scooter. Scooter steals food. Scooter takes the most comfortable cat bed. Scooter hides the catnip pillows. I don't know why there's a cat fight going on upstairs right now, but I know who's to blame. It's the third time this week. I wonder if Mr. Snooze or Tippy is the victim today.

"Sarah! Stop those cats this instant!" yells Mom from the kitchen.

"I'm trying!" she says. "I could use some help!"

"This is your problem. You deal with it," says Mom. That's Mom's approach to teenagers. They make their own messes. They should clean them up. I decide to help, though. I can't bear the thought of two well-behaving cats being pummeled by that bully.

"Here, take Mr. Snooze," Sarah says when I reach the top of the stairs. She scruffs him away from Scooter and tosses him my direction. Good thing he's small or I'd have tumbled backwards down the stairs because she threw him so hard. Poor cat. Poor me having Sarah for a sister.

When I get to my room I slam the door shut and lay Mr. Snooze on my bed. I examine his body for fresh blood but don't find any, not this time. Last Monday's fight was a lot worse when I caught Scooter in mid-flight as he was about to pounce on Mr. Snooze for the third time in a game of tag, only Mr. Snooze wasn't even playing. What a one-sided, unfair match!

"It's okay, Mr. Snooze," I say. "Mom will reach her breaking point soon. That nasty old cat will have to get a new home, one without pets *or* kids *or* maybe with *any* people for that matter. *Hmph!* As I am petting Mr. Snooze,

I feel a bump near his ear on his head. He seems uncomfortable when my fingers touch it lightly. I run my hand over the bump again. Pressing the bump gently the most disgusting stuff starts oozing out of it. It is thick and yellowish with blood. I start to gag as I smell a terrible odor.

"Mom!" I shout. "We have a problem!" Since I'm not the child causing alarm unnecessarily, Mom comes running to my room.

"What's the matter?" she asks, out of breath.

"Mr. Snooze has a nasty bump that's oozing some very nasty stuff out of it. Look." I point to the spot on his head.

"Did you just find it?"

"Yes."

"It's Scooter's fault," she says through gritted teeth.

"I don't know, Mom. I don't think it's a new bump."

"Okay. Go find the cat carrier. Put Mr. Snooze in there for safe keeping. I'll see if the veterinarian has an opening this afternoon."

*****

If you were the veterinarian, what would you do next? Make a list of Mr. Snooze's injuries. Then make a diagnostic (treatment) plan based upon the information that you have. When you are done, read what the veterinarian will do.

Name of the Animal (patient):

Type of Animal:

Symptoms or Injuries:

Treatment:

History:

*The owner noticed a soft, oozing mass on the head.

*Mr. Snooze has been fighting with another cat recently.

Assessment:

*Mr. Snooze has a low grade fever.

*There is an abscess on his head. An abscess is a pocket of pus that forms near an old bite or scratch wound. It is a collection of bacteria, white blood cells, and red blood cells. In other words, an abscess is an infected area under the skin. This abscess is draining.

Treatment Plan:

*If the abscess was not already draining, the doctor would have to sedate the cat and then surgically get the abscess to drain. If an abscess does not drain, it will be difficult to treat even with a medication.

*Mr. Snooze is sent home with an oral antibiotic. This will help the cat fight off the bacteria that are causing the infection.

*The owner is instructed to "hot pack" the wound multiple times a day. The owner will apply a warm, wet wash cloth to the wound to help keep it draining for a few days.

*****

I wish I could say that Scooter behaves himself now, but that would be a lie. He's still a brat. However, Mom put her foot down with Sarah. Scooter is only allowed in the basement or Sarah's room. Mr. Snooze and Tippy haven't received any new injuries. And truth be told, early in the morning before school, sometimes I sneak down to the basement to tell Scooter *good-bye*. Do you know what that cat does when he's got no one to show off in front of or no one to torment? He actually purrs and rubs his head against my leg. I admit he has kind of grown on me. Don't tell my sister.

Dr. Ed Blesy graduated from the University of Illinois College of Veterinary Medicine in 1997. In 2006 he opened his own clinic, St. Joseph Animal Wellness Clinic, in Southwest Michigan. He has appeared on-air with Wild Bill on 97.5FM radio to answer listeners' vet questions and written pet-related articles for *Lakeside Family Magazine*. He and his wife Marcy enjoy spending time on the beautiful beaches of Lake Michigan and attending the activities of their two sons. Dr. Blesy can be reached via his website or Facebook page at sjvet.com.

Marcy Blesy is the author of several middle grade and young adult novels. Her picture book, *Am I Like My Daddy?*, helps children who experienced the loss of a parent when they were much younger. She has also been published in two *Chicken Soup for the Soul* books as well as various newspapers and magazines. By day she runs an elementary school library and enjoys spending time with her husband Ed and two boys.

Check out *Be the Vet, Part 2.*

Follow our facebook page for more specific information.

We would love an Amazon review as well. Thank you for your time.

Other Children's Books by Marcy Blesy:

Evie and the Volunteers Series

Join ten-year-old Evie and her friends as they volunteer all over town meeting lots of cool people and getting into just a little bit of trouble. There is no place left untouched by their presence, and what they get from the people they meet is greater than any amount of money.

Book 1   Animal Shelter

Book 2   Nursing Home

Book 3   After-School Program

Book 4   Coming November 2016

49809415R00041

Made in the USA
San Bernardino, CA
05 June 2017